A Blue Woman

&

Warren II & The Return of Mr Zane

A Blue Woman

&

Warren II & The Return of Mr Zane

Harry Stefano

THE REGENCY
PUBLISHERS

ISBN: 979-8-9909505-1-1 (Paperback Edition)
ISBN: 979-8-9909505-2-8 (Hardcover Edition)
ISBN: 979-8-9909505-0-4 (E-book Edition)

Book Ordering Information

The Regency Publishers, US
521 5th Ave 17th floor NY, NY10175
Phone Number: (315)537-3088 ext 1007
Email: info@theregencypublishers.com
www.theregencypublishers.com

Printed in the United States of America

Contents

INTRODUCTION

When I was growing up as a child I actually tended to wear an awful lot of the colour 'blue'- it was not necessarily that I was making a statement; in fact it was not for years later that this was indeed noted and pointed out to me. Blue denim was one of my wardrobe staples during this rather hectic period in my life. And Nowadays I tend to associate 'blue' with those in the medical profession- more specifically 'nurses'- as part of their uniform attire- navy and blue. It`s funny `cos some nurses I tend to never actually see in their everyday clothing- I guess this is all part of the professional distancing these days which when considering things like 'what is capacity?' must be observed at all times. Switching from a Hospital environment into the community was a bit different – majorly so- adjusting and adapting to fit effectively new environments always held its own set of new problems. And I couldn`t quite manage to effectively do away without any kind of support at all. I bore no shame I this- since mental health whilst still a relatively 'shunned' topic on the agenda was beginning to be more and more talked about. This however did not necessarily mean instant acceptance. I think particularly when considering things like the 'equality' concept- since how could an individual like myself be accepted into the community- or society as a whole- without firstly trying to become involved and actively participate to an extent. I still had to recall some invaluable advise from a great CPN- that is how one must remember one`s limitations- especially with a mental health condition- this was on another memorable day for me involving job search- yet again. I always remained optimistic for my future when considering how I continued with my academic qualifications to date- as a useful tool for proving further my capacity as an individual- as well as gaining work experience. Anyhow, I remained optimistic and excited to see exactly what the jobs market would 'throw' at me this time! Hahahahahaha- it always proved an interesting time! I would sometimes be held on section- detained- in hospital- and still be searching for a job! Hahahahaha. My strong will and determination to continue onwards with not only my life- but my career effectively- most definitely paid off in the long run. By this time I had reached a major decision that I was no longer interested in becoming a nurse. I realised the ever more pressing need to effectively seek further freedom and independence from which a job could provide me with- as well as the god forsaken awful mess it could further get me into! All the more reason to effectively fill my day- as one thing I had in abundance- was time on my hands! I just could not go on pottering- with mundane household tasks- and knew I would never make a house goddess! (Especially since I hired in cleaners routinely to clean for me). Nowadays I found myself with a somewhat pocket full of debt effectively- and trying to problem solve- in order to better manage. This was a real test of living skills for me indeed. In this particular chapter of my career path- I had exhausted my level of stress management- as well as my level of personal fitness for this particular role. I indeed felt comforted by the notion of how this particular jobs role was a young persons` game these days! Hahahahaha. This did not prevent me though from continuing onwards with a more gentler exercise fitness regieme.

Well as usual- in my love life- nothing really worked out- or went according to plan- not exactly anyway. Blondie soon deserted me- and went off to romp onwards with some local flussie! Much to my horror and disgust (but I reckon I handled it all rather well at the time) since he decided to pay me an unexpected 'visit' of sorts with no real shame or concern for me- complete with flussie in tow. I just couldn't and didn't speak to him. It just highlighted further his total lack of respect for me- as well as it was an old 'trick' played on me by a former boyfriend; many years ago- I knew not to get involved. I thought what a cheek- now that we had in actual fact had intercourse many moons ago- he knew I still held a torch for him- up until that point. I thought it was a dirty rotten trick to play being as I was on route to work my night shift- and I once more decided not to make a great fuss. Since this was indeed his choice totally. Now that he had made his decision with this flussie- who looked as thin as a rake as well as probably on drugs together- the pair did not look well anyway. But in time it indeed worked- in that he did me a favour in how- I could now make plans to move on- easily so whilst remembering the hirt and pain which he tried to cause me. No way was I going to be absorbed in a relationship whereby I would be routinely abused subject to the whims of an ass! For the following week I saw that he was chasing someone else! Abominable- he didn't seem to care at all about me- this just further proved exactly how insane he was to me by his totally wreckless actions. And I reckon that it would only be a matter of time before he would be gaining a reputation in the community for the equivalent of a male slag effectively. For what did he want? I don't think that even he knew what he wanted. No way would I follow suit to be like him- quite frankly more deeper thinking took hold. Knowing how he used cheap flusies like this by once telling me how he liked to fuck! Well obviously without reading too deeply into this- I wasn't the first woman he had hurt- especially since counting on one hand how he was already onto no: 3! Meanwhile as for myself I retained my self respect- and would not be pressured into performing sexual acts in order to satisfy the unhinged! For if it wasn't love- then simply I didn't want to know any more.

Mr Zane did make an attempt at re entering my life- but I just recounted all the emotional upset this could potentially lead to. And besides it just didn`t make any sense to get back together effectively. I know he thought my long and didtant silence was a means of punishing him to an extent. But anyway I could forgive him a little for wanting something that he could never provide – total happiness with him! Instead Mr Zane continued to be on the outskirts of my newly found freedom and life.

Indeed a rather bleak dry spell in my life- just fuelled me with yet more time on my hands to adjust and make necessary improvements. I call this phase- `project self`- and whilst I went through yet another makeover- keeping up my beauty facials and ensuring I undertook some gentle exercise- things just got more and more nastier with blondie as well as his colleagues! We are talking about smashed up windows, screaming and shouting in the streets- he was sending a seriously nasty message to me and the people locally! As this impacted and took hold somewhat I had to stay away from the pool facility for the foreseeable at least. As fighting was breaking out all over. Once more false allegations were made- having discovered that I was in fact in a sort of relationship with another of these men! I came off the worst- and there was nothing that could be done or said for that matter. All I know is that Blondie turned out to be a really nasty piece of work.

Anyway years went by and I remained single but hopeful and optimistic that Mr Right was indeed waiting for me and out there. Anyway after much waiting- and trials and tribulations he turned up. He was a mature man- and we only ever met and saw each other in secret. It was at just the time when my ego needed a little boosting. After much in the way of mantras to oneself consisting of idealogical fantasies etc- and many therapy sessions to date. All of which helped to an extent- or was I indeed pouring petrol on the flames?! Anyway it provided a good opportunity to talk- and by goodness I swore – a lot! Hahahahahaha. He was Mr Perfect- perfect because of how he looked and what he said just had be captivated for an absolute age! He was a man who I instantly fell for- and I guess part of me was holding back because I wanted to get it right this time. My personal sterio headset already played wedding music! Despite my strong woman appeal I still harboured a softer more gentile side occasionally wanting a perfect life scenario of a blissful wedding! However would this be a piece of paper all glorified for historical purposes? Was I scared?- oh absolutely! Hahahahahahaha Still I had to question the whole concept of romance

OMG! My 'most recent new' ideal man was turning into a complete nightmare already. Naturally he had one hell of a face (for a man)- perfectly chiselled in every way- with great cheek bones. And today he was boasting a new haircut to boot! This was indeed the almighty problem- I could never actually pin anyone down these days- exchanging telephone numbers was virtually unheard of! Anyway I resided to my previous thinking- of how simply if they didn't want to be with me – they were indeed nuts! Looking for some action I discovered a two cans of rose cider in my depleated fridge- and cracked one open- I couldn't believe it I begun to drink and round the corner came a police vehicle! Hahahahaha – this was indeed my own living premises- I was well above the drinking age to consume alcohol- so today I succumbed to one whole can of cider.

My love-life was completely down the swanny once more- and do you know how to actually get your own back- as a means of fighting onwards with one's demons –particularly when they refuse to converse or see you anymore? Was I something I'd done? Absolutely not- but hey everyone it would appear had an axe to grind of sorts with me actually being in a relationship these days- jealousy was not the word! After going through stages of completely pissed off- to utter sadness on times- thank god I skipped the angry phase and then came to my senses! It would seem that the worst punishment one can pursue is to essentially just be Okay- show the entire world- that you are I fact okay! Really- and above all else continue to look after oneself. I was still waiting for the next prince to sweep me off my feet- for I deserved no less than treatment fit for a princess! Instead what did I get other than the manners of an ape it would seem! Here I was a beautiful, intelligent woman nowadays being treated like a piece of shit essentially- how dare he. All I could do in my efforts to retain my ego- was to consider all my positive points- and how I quite simply could not be compared to most women. Sine my lifes path was indeed quite different- as I recently explained I still remain surrounded by a sphere of mental health to date- with increasingly more emphasis being upon my remaining well! Yes granted I knew I was different- but this is what made me mental- as in a mental health service user. In fact these days I was soooo different- that I could only accommodate/stand the company of other individuals within the mental health system of sorts! If I didn't get on with someone- I no longer had time for them. You see being a service user I over the years had received plenty of time to draw on all the information provided to me- so now what was once perceived to be a weakness- then became my strength these days! I managed to turn the whole thing on its head effectively. To the point of being empowered by this very knowledge- what I knew- the mental health education I received over the years was indeed priceless! My insight was great- to the point where it frightened others- or so it seemed to! Hahahahahahaha

After being institutionalised for a fair bit really within a mental health system which I once loathed- I grew to love in fact. The thing of it was that people could these days 'see' that I was in fact different to them- and I was. I was often described as odd or different- and it was funny – because I viewed some people as odd these days too. And yes I was different I was a mental health service user! I couldn't help it- I was mental! Hhahahahahah (like it or lump it)- my condition was never going too go away. Did it hold me back from life? Sometimes- but it just depended on how determined I was to succeed if not win- in a given situation for a desired outcome. Careerwise things were on the up- somewhat-however one had to consider the limitations of medication combined with my condition. In reality my private life alongside local slander continuing and social stigma surrounding mental health conditions was a real battle- particularly if one could avoid this- ie through assuming anonymity regarding ones` condition for instance. It was funny too since I only really tended to fit in with those who were in the mental health sphere themselves- be it as a patient or worker- these days still despite the equality act- relationships with a mental health service user was still frowned upon in society. We know that relationships went on- because of all the adopted children as a further indication of how society was not going to tolerate in reality individuals within mental health- perceiving themselves to be of a better breed than 'us'! And these days it really did feel that way too- 'them' and 'us'! Horrible stories still circulated about paedophelia etc- (these ignorant people were in no certain terms- asking for the death penalty to be re-instated)- it was horrific. Even being targeted for one`s finances- `cos do you know what- they simply didn`t care about us- denied midwifery care- on the NHS- would your believe?! In reality we were simply here for those to abuse- if they could- Isolation and lonliness was always on the cards- simply because of who we were – mental! So addressing that age old question: how does one make a good quality of life for oneself- when secretly that old society were in fact organising 'geneside' of sorts- we knew this- one didn`t have to be paranoid to recognise when others were deliberately being difficult towards us- hence this lead to as they knew only too well increased use of meds and another spell in the institution – all for their gratification- as this impact served to further work on one`s kidneys too- physically taking its toll as well as mentally. Was I scarred from my experience within the institution? Not really- it was a serious dealing- however I developed cognitive better life coping skills over time. I had to combat 'it' this inherent societal problem with mental health- as well as learning how to 'speak out' effectively and be heard- Hey I was born here- how dare you say

I have no rights- and a second class citizen effectively! No matter how long in terms of considering how things would improve over time- did change really happen? Instead they provided a list of excuses- this just provided the green light for their mistreatment of us.

Anyway, Blondie and I had actually fallen out as it were- and the entire town were aware of this it would seem. It didn`t take much- and believe me my new found success and freedom was somewhat enraging him- to the point of utter envy. I tried to smooth things over- but nothing could persuade him. It would seem that we had reached an understanding in that we were now 'friends' and he decided to reject the baby (love-child) that was growing inside me. I don`t know what happened to him- but over time as the years passed- and I needed to once more throw myself into the world of work – we just grew apart- or at least the distance between us became more noticeable indeed- in fact these days I only saw him when he turned up to insult me of sorts- it was terrible the ongoing onslaught of abuse- determined as ever no way was I going to have an abortion- no fucking way! Besides he was simply a sperm donor- we both knew what we were doing and entered into a verbal contract of sorts. I was a good mother- of course I was- and couldn`t wait for the birth of my baby. To share in the joys and pleasures bestowed on a family like Christmas time and enjoying the Summer etc. Blondie would never accept how much I deep down cared for him and was not willing to reciprocate these feelings.

The dark underworld of prostitution had caught up with me once more- it was most definitely a realm which I would never entertain the idea of- and so I needed to keep myself safe uttermost- since this underworld served to take away everything that I had worked for. I everyday clung to my mother- especially when these pimps continued to circulate my address and whereabouts. The only thing I could do in effect to escape and for my personal security was to hold on tightly to my education in the making. It`s what us big girls did to getaway in effect from these disgusting excuses for women. This dark underworld wanted to take us under- everyday- they seethed to the point of challenging us as we walked the streets with total freedom- but minful of the dangers ever present by their existence- nothing could be done- as educated women like myself we were called ugly- and how we should be subservient to men our counterparts- an educated pretty face these days some women just wanted to scratch out our eyes! I was a full grown woman- still hunted by these lesser beings- and just a little anecdote which occurred the other day- in ofference of support but still highlighting my fragile situation within society- it made me laugh- but it was indeed a serious message to me as well. A rather tall handsomely dressed man whilst on route with his family noticing the rather cretins of people being obnoxious towards me whilst motoring past and getting an eye full of me in my very much sought after flat in a very prestigious area- stuck up for me for a change- (one had to be there) it was a symbol very much of class essentially- indicative of them and us- highlighting how in as much as they didn`t give a shit about me/us- we ought not to spare their feelings too- anyway he proceeded to make a gesture with his smart jacket and mouthed to the passing traffic- so that they would understand- 'do you want some money mate?!'- anyway it was a real snobbery hoot- and designed to offend too- just reminding all concerned of our current situation and outlook perhaps furthermore on things. It delighted me- and knowing that he most definitely shared empathy towards my dilemma- we both knew full well that they simply wanted what 'we' had in fact. There was safety in helping oneself it would seem- and no room for the vulnerable- not in this game of survival and utter tactics.

It came as quite a 'blow' to see how completely 'taken-over' yet how stupid Blondie was- since a latest argument had presented some very misguided thinking indeed- yes we were indeed fighting/arguing- and I determined to be myself as always. Our latest spat was how he decided to tell me that- he had been told of my childishness! Would you believe it- something which he clearly didn`t understand. I vermy much disliked being referred to as an 'image' of sorts (just to clarify this is indeed a term to define part of a mental health condition indicated by presenting as a 'child'- when in fact an adult). This descriptor of me as a youthful woman most definitely infuriated me since- they had watched me as an avid partygoer- upperclass- something which they would never begin to understand- in no way did I have 'learning difficulties'- and I wasn`t prepared to role reversal with my own mother! Yes sometimes whilst enjoying a joke or two I could be rather 'silly'- but how dare he begin to chastise me- I could be forgiven for- those in my company seemed to share my humour- the main thing was once more I was being judged!? I was such a popular partygoer- and everyone shared my enthusiasm- and loved my party frocks! Hahahahahahaha. A little popularity perhaps- indeed went a long way- and please don`t tell me how to be! The main thing was that I was indeed out of Hospital- and still very much compliant with my medication- there were sooooo many jealous people of 'us' upperclass somewhat- thinking that they could indeed replace me?! Clutching at straws they were in efforts to try to take away my independence and freedom- I 'roared' "…No way Bitch/Bastard!" For you would seriously have to 'kill' me first! Hahahahahahaha These backard women I felt had had the rule of the roost and their way for far too long. I knew too my only ways forward for survival since I loathed 'that lot' so much was to continue making large strides within my academic studies- and let my hair down I will! Hahahahahahahaha

I decided to rather embrace my mental health 'straight-jacket'- since shame on 'him' not me- and darling- over the years- he had not grown any kinder! Nor had mother nature bestowed on him even finer looks- he was indeed- getting 'old'! Good bye then! Chaw! Please darling don`t give me excuses- an indication of my blessed looks were indeed the sheer scale of the ongoing 'fighting'!

Hahahahahaha- all done with the critique- I slowly gave up on him- besides- he was no fun at all! Ham and chips went down quite nicely this suppertime!- no way would I flippin` die of heartache any longer for someone who didn`t quite appreciate me as an individual!- And I vowed no man would ever put me off my food!- I quite simply continued to look after myself- which is what they hated me for! Hahahahahahaha

This Summer I missed the smell of the swimming pool- I love it the fresh smell of the chlorine- but it would appear how there had been a whole new set of problems with my frequenting the swimming pool. Once more I was under 'attack' for my private life. And rumours were indeed circulating of how I was supposedly a lesbian!? Simply because I was remaining both faithful to my boyfriend as well as out of self respect I was these days celibate- but not for want of 'offers'- and I was not prepared to settle for any old yanto/man in order to satisfy my personal sexual desires. A great many of my ex boyfriends who were indeed jealous of my new found social standing- as an independent empowered woman- needed to justify why these days I rejected them- I had moved onwards- and all for how they did not behave in the way/ fashion that I wanted them. I was accustomed to Guernsey men- whereby everything just happened- and it was 'right' too! These male counter-parts couldn`t stand the female friendships that I had forged too- and yes it was my way of saying how I would continue to please myself- for after being alienated by former social circles- I made my own way ahead with better and a far stronger peer group- what gutted most male counterparts was my independence and strength as a woman- it was like OMG how dare she live alone- they needed me to perish in a rather competitive society.

I just found it rather childish nowadays to be considered as a lesbian- knowing full well that I was a straight/heterosexual woman- they hated how I could in fact rise above shit- and look anyone in the eyes- as an equal of sorts! And what business was it my private affairs- to them anyway?! And I defy any woman to boast of having been in bed with moi! Hahahahahahahahahaha- because that woman would indeed be a liar! It didn`t help my sporting good-looks either- but I make no apologies- for I remain straight/heterosexual forever- anatomy and physiology is the name of the game- fools! Hahahahahahahahaha

All I will say is that quite an impression had formed of me- and another 'studmuffin' was most definitely within my sights- at least- obviously I had intrigued him somewhat- For HE CAME HE SAW- I CONQUERED! Hahahahahaha- and a big triumph indeed- (big waves in small ways)- he had the face and body to live for- myself what a perfect match-for I too was tall in statue- and he continued to fascinate me after this – our first encounter! Yet not enough to totally go overboard- and knock myself out- I was playing it 'cool'! hahahahahahaha

Just because I was currently single- did not make me a desperate woman- instead it made me more determined to get what I wanted. I found the rather dull pool-men now a bit like old 'pee-wees'- just no longer cool- or fun to be around. I should have noted the rather boring choice of clothing- grey marl jogging suits!- My life of fashion continued and I didn`t want to end up like them! I feel that the status-quo had swallowed them up- sometimes one has to indeed fight for one`s right to party! Instead I found comfort and solice in the arms of the educated and elite! Sick to death of trying soooo hard with someone who was simply too thick to realise my talents as a woman. I simply had a rather unique measuring tool these days- for measuring a person- and I needed to feel appreciated in every way- which just disgusted me more and more- his behaviour and warped sense of humour.

The concept of marriage- remained a total mystery to me- for I never to this day truly bought into it- having worked within the hotel industry- it was both a mockery and hypocritical. And besides I had no real 'use' for a husband- someone to argue with?! For I enjoyed my independence too much- answerable to myself alone! However recently I did joke to my mum in relation to how if I decided to get married today it would be a small registry office job- and then back down to earth with a 'bump' of sorts. I simply didn't find it confident- going around like most married couples within my society stating- how they were married- it was like this gave them an excuse to leave the rest of the human race- if you get my drift- it gave them a reason to fight for their wives- as well as how pathetic as this would seem- it was barbaric and uneducated- it was a very working-class thing to do I felt. Since I felt the need to respond to these assholes by citing regularly – how I was a single independent woman- and feel empowered enough by this! Hahahahahahahahaha- for my single status did not hold me back- and besides I knew precisely what it was- my mental health condition- and as long as I continued to take my medication- this pissed them off and do you know what- 'good'- because for years they had succeeded in pissing me off! Still waiting for Mr Right- and already my little ripples were beginning to be felt- for never before had there been such an independent woman! Not in this small town anyway! Hahahahahahahahahaha I just simply refused to listen any longer- especially when I considered them to be less than equal to myself and in many ways lacking. To date I feel ones' personal curriculum vitae is a rather good indication/ measure of a person- and this is essentially how I survived.

OMG I was actually getting older- much older- and I needed a little pick me up from time to time just to stop myself from entering into chronic boredom or depression- I also needed to stop telling others my personal problems and treating almost anyone as a private councillor- although I admit I wasn't that bad- I felt I was a figure of much cheeriness and joy- but as I once stated- I am only human! And sick of thers treating me like a punch bag- and outpouring their problems- I thought no I refuse to suffer in silence any longer- not that I was complaining- but others seemed to get away with it! Hahahahahahaha Anyway I really had to keep a check on this negative behaviour and felt like counselling was a very mean tool indeed- `cos I simply didn`t want to dwell on things. I managed to remain upbeat as always- this was the only way to fight this evil phenomenon sweeping the city- a culture of really moaning people and depressing with it! Despite living apart from Blondie I always seemed to channel my thoughts towards him regularly- it was incredible we were two different people living separate lives yet we were indeed both in love! Hahahahahahaha I knew it and he felt it- I knew he did! In fact by his very being there in my presence- I knew he cared! And the best part f it was that we never argued. I`d like sit in my plush flat and think right then- what would Blondie do now/say now if I dared to consume alcohol or a cigarette for that matter?! Hahahahahaha And yes in much of my spare time I would indeed obsess over him- which I`m sure he was well aware of! I wrote to him from time to time too- hey this is 'me'! Hahahahahahaha And causing I big commotion I did! How resourceful since we found other ways/places to be together. When I was broke and staying in as it were- I was with him- in fact almost everywhere I went- I was with 'him'. Was I possessive? Hell yes indeed! Hahahahahahaha- and it seemed like he was too- to a point- although we hadn`t actually gotton into bed yet- we were getting there! Besides this mad frenzy which he would have me in was all the more fun! Only he did ever have this effect on me! Cool and careful we most definitely had to be – since our old haunts had been 'discovered' and I was giving nothing away! But determined to play the part- and so was he a willing party too- Lovers` lane just got more attractive- and essentially moved away from the old Orchards that were the initial spot- as it got completely ruined for both of us by others mainly – so became less appealing! I just needed to see him and hear his words of encouragement- enough to orgasm metaphorically speaking! Hahahahahahaha It was worth it believe me! I was sooo driven by him- he was well aware! And we couldn`t stop ourselves essentially.

It became an all to awful 'trick' of reality to dismiss my beautiful good looks and easy temperament along with my unmistakingly inteliigence- with cretins claiming that I was mentally ill. All too often this was their first line of defence against me- for unfortunately I could not go on living anonymously (by this I mean without people knowing how I had a mental health label)- they thought this would indeed cover everything and therefore then they could prey effectively on not only making themselves feel better but 'outcompete' me in the marriage market as it was. I gave up watching the television to date because their image of perfectionism of how people were supposed to look- and how they determined to dictate this on the big screen disgusted me! I will argue how size 6 became quickly and overnight the social norm- and real women like myself who after seeing a lot of life experience were in fact very much belittled in a big way. Nevermind the fact that we were educated- in order to separate ourselves from the animals in effect. Following advise we had taken our medication and freedom and independence came at a most inconvenient price still. For one seriously had to be a strong woman of sorts to outmanouvre this lot. Effectively jobs and education were the way forward. And my thoughts on aesthetic improvements and cosmetic surgery to date remain firm in that in no way will I entertain more than a simple facial. Not whilst I still had a healthy radiance about me. A recent conversation which I had with mum outlined more sound reasoning for not having cosmetic surgery since one could not fool mother nature. I explained to mum how an actor had recently passed away and he almost looked disfigured from having his plastic surgery- I said to mum that there is no easy cheat or quick fix to obtaining good lasting looks and overall health! And a healthy regieme is something which is time consuming and needs to be started relatively early in life through education ongoing for instance. Mum agreed. I'd recently overheard bits and pieces of a discussion in a local pub for a couple who the woman was in fact planning some sorts of plastic surgery- and they were in fact discussing how they were going to pay for this. My judgement today is that anybody who wants you to have plastic surgery and encourages a person in this- quite simply doesn`t love you!? I still to this day consider myself to be very fortunate in my genetic makeup and I established a routine basic beauty regime from an early age- since my Nan was a model back in the day and was already advising me on my use of a good moisturser! Rightly or wrongly so. That was an era whereby it was considered as extreme and overboard to encourage young women I beauty pagents however these days I think it is all too punishing in itself to encourage the use of plastic surgery if not damaging to the individual psychologically. Yes I can indeed boast to date that all my looks are one hundred percent natural- I also was fortunate in following a sportswoman route in cycling, jogging and swimming which kept old age at bay somewhat and I effectively had turned the clock back in terms of considering my real age- for I was told recently once more that I looked half my age! Hahahahahahahahaha The great competition goes on- within warring families and wider society- for the better looking and more intelligent/successful woman! It`s dog-eat dog and very cruel on times- as I always say: all is indeed fair one way or another! And yes if two people want to be together then they will- in reality not to be brushed under the carpet affairs happen and are created effectively- no one can stop this!

Being such a good-looking woman like myself- it most definitely had it`s pitfalls. Everyone wanting to know more about my private life for instance. And there were many who dreamt of having my happiness and set about to wreck this effectively- my lovelife. Yes I have to say that being a mental health service user- people were all to ready to dismiss me- I never thought i`d reach the point of being soooo fucking intimidating once more in regards to my personal looks and sheer intellect! Hahahahahahahaha . I wasn`t prepared to give them a second chance to prove exactly how nasty they were towards me- they just imagined if they got enough people to lie effectively about me- slander- knowing full well it would never go to court- but just enough to do 'damage' to my good name! And I had no protection from this scorn of evil and wrath of the shunned. Hence secrecy was always a must in order to secure something meaningful and lasting- I resented others poking their noses into my private life in order to help themselves effectively. And the police would only serve to help the rich- and family memebers- yes in effect I`m saying the Police were there for those who could pay. There were many that I worked with over the years who were terrified of the police- and I just couldn`t help thinking why this was exactly? I never dared to probe any deeper though on any level. Because I knew of the great bother I had been involved in over the years with the police and fortunately my looks saved me there! Hahahahahahahaha Yes I can recall now a few of them were I fact terrified of the police! Whereas myself I came into contact with them regularly- there were even rumours circulating of how I was part of CID! Hahahahahahahahaha I think had it not been for how successful I was they really would not have tolerated me- and there were a few who I know didn`t personally like me- and they made no quarms in showing this distaste towards me. I didn`t have to be paranoid to know that the police were in fact around 5 minutes away from any given location in the city with their stations everywhere it would seem.

OMG How I longed every day for Blondie but we both had to be careful- there were too many prying eyes. And yes his absence only made me long for him more and more. It was only the other day that I was told how I had a 'banging face' which I took as such a great compliment. I know he wondered about me too from time to time and he knew where I lived and sometimes he knew my whereabouts when I was out walking and taking some gentle exercise so that we could both meet up effectively and just gaze at each other lovingly.

Fighting with 'traffic' became another strange phenomenon for me- since random people were hell bent on telling me there thoughts regardless – by this I mean most of them did not know me-and the things they said sometimes was outrageous- beyond belief! I really had to learn to control myself in these sometimes awkward situations- I noticed though there were one or two who would fall victim to talking to the traffic in their feeble attempts to communicate and express themselves I guess- but I on the other hand found this amusing to a degree- it was like 'playing with traffic' and not in a good way- thoroughly lunacy unless of coarse I spotted someone that I actually knew- it was soooo surreal and too weird for words on times! Hahahahahahahahaha. Although I was a popular figure in the community it was freaky some of the people who claimed to be in a relationship with me! Hahahahahahahahaha

One can still see me waiting for Blondie to return home in my window balcony of sorts- annoying almost all my neighbours now- no I`m not gawking at you with my cup of tea- it`s just any excuse to get some much needed fresh air as well as eye candy! Hahahahahahahahaha And I`ve gotten into all sorts of bother for this new past time- even to the point whereby people have been thinking that I have been spying on them- would you believe?! Hahahahahahaha- I was told recently to mind my own business- and to explain myself?! Hahahahahahahaha. The only thing I haven`t done I that window is get naked and I did rather have to stop myself from flashing on the odd occasion- it was too irresistible! Hahahahahahahaha. Which reminds me I do not regret sending rude pics recently to Blondie- anyway my cleavage was very accentuated as well as the mask provided for my face quite tastefully done- (I gave him a mask as a present recently too). Which reminds me that we may have to round with masks on- it`ll be easier- (private joke)!

Was I truly happy like this? Oh absolutely- everything was an effort- eg to see my boyfriend I needed to do battle with many things- and outwit most- his work colleagues had caught wind of our little relationship too! Which had it`s own challenges and little surprises- to the point of how it just gave them the green light to be rude towards me on occasion- oh and was I a 'good' slut!? They made their feelings plain in their efforts to split us up effectively or at the very least not support our little relationship. It became fucking obvious over time though- that I was indeed involved- if not because I just kept my legs crossed- yes for me he was the 'one'! I particularly enjoyed the inconvenience of it- as well as the convenience of it- I was such a practical woman I guess- yet I was no domestic goddess- and still enjoyed the night life/ partying I forgave him for his double life and he allowed me my little idiosyncrasies! Everytime we met it was like our two worlds collided- and the entire fucking town knew! It was the perfect mutual arrangement of sorts- and seemed to suit us both no end. Were we prepared to go to the next level? Oh sleeping with each other- well that would spoil things for the moment- the foreplay was fucking amazing! Hahahahahahaha And so here we both are encapsulated in time- our time as it is- and annoying as others may find us- yes we are in love!

It was the year 2023 and so far I had been on the run so to speak for a good number of years- I like to pretend that Warren was indeed my guardian angel. How wrong I was…It would appear that at this stage sperm donor extraordinaire was all that Warren would ever amount to being in my life. And I had got exactly what I had wanted, so to speak. So serves me right for finding that all I had prepared/planned/hoped for had actually taken shape. I knew that Warren would never commit to me in any more formal way; I screamed "Alrite I get it! I`m on my own with this one- well and truly!" I felt all mixture of emotions happy and then somewhat a little disappointed. But I was a grown up- and by this time had learned that the only way forward was indeed to stand on my own two feet, and cope effectively. Afterall one night of getting exactly what I had wanted had now changed my life forevermore! Here I was now heavily pregnant and Warren was in fact nowhere to be seen! Twas only on one separate occasion that I had seen Warren- and he rather tactfully told me: how I had become fat, and that he loved his wife! I instantly grew upset with this new revelation; afterall who wouldn`t- he wasn`t thinking about me at all it would seem; only himself. Warren turned out to be a very welcome impregnation- however he made it quite clear how he simply needed to `close the door` on me then- like as though we never were. Was he being selfish- or was I? Yes he just wanted his cake and to eat it- without anyone finding out in the process. I knew I had to effectively survive from here on in on my own- with my baby. I must stress that in no way did I have any regrets about now having his lovechild. And absolutely I had got precisely what I wanted. A shock to the system that he meant every word of what he had said to me- and left me effectively to continue with his own life. Which did provide a massive shock to the system for me, and some getting used to- for the one thing that I could depend on was that he was never going to be there for me. Was I happy? Oh without question. But the whole cruel nature of a very backward society entrenched in a backward tradition of time held beliefs etc, was not going to go away overnight.

Yes Warren really had to cover his tracks in efforts to protect himself and his lifestyle that he had become accustomed to. One Summers` day I happened to `bump` into Warrens` family- well what exactly happened was that it turns out his wife now on this particular day had no less than a brood of around 6 children with her down at the local beachside not too far from where Warren worked. I nearly `died`! However, I could see that he had been one busy man- and she did make a point to acknowledge me in a negative way- because it would seem that she did know about me. I couldn`t help thinking: my God: How could anyone agree to have that many children?! Obviously their marriage was on the rocks again/once more- and as the old saying goes- a baby will either make or break a relationship/marriage. I truly believe that this is what she felt she needed to do- in order to `keep` Warren so to speak. And I remember thinking to myself well she was a rather thin woman in statue- and I felt a little sorry for her. It was as if she was saying- now look what I`ve had to do- type of thing!? Warren was no where to be seen on this occasion. I then proceeded to be deep in thought for around a few days. Just pondering on what I had seen? My God, he now had all these children- just like in the old-fashioned days gone by. And at one stage my regards switched towards the mothers` welfare itself- for how could she possibly function as a woman or as an individual for that matter? She had a very restrictive mothering role now to perform I felt- speaking as a highliy ambitious and motivated woman myself. It wasn`t until the following year that shock number three/four was to emerge it would seem.

It was by chance, and it was over the New Years` festive period- and I rememeber thinking to myelf- my God how dare they mock me- and my efforts- for I had landed in a nice two bedroom flat- enough provision for me and my little one that I was expecting. Whilst I wasn`t overly rich or poor I found city living just allowed me to fade into the background sometimes; which I enjoyed with my privacy being important to me. I couldn`t understand a few things though?

Anyway, I hopped onto a free bus service that took me into the coast on route to the bay. I was just trying to enjoy some time out and away from the flat for a time. And suddenly it struck me- the bus took a turn in the road, and there it was; so blazingly obvious- a camper/trailer park of sorts, complete with travellers! I had accidentally stumbled upon where they now resided/lived it would seem! I took the oportuntity to think once more; but it was not about Warrens` living circumstances. Instead I turned myself to the more pressing issue of my private finances.

I pressed on for as long as I could really; leaving little monies over from my dwindling income; which consequently lead to considerably more borrowing in order to sustain the lifestyle in which I had become accustomed to. I didn`t really consider myself to be living an extravagant lifestyle of sorts. But there was now an even greater dip in the economy; and everyone was feeling the pinch. The more I cut back; the more resourceful I became. My main priority was indeed my baby' and addressing basic needs i.e food, heat and clothing really. Life became increasingly difficult, and holidays were in fact well and truly off the agenda for the foreseeable. I did for a considerable period conceal my debts from all; including my mum. And then as more time went on it became a little more difficult to keep up with it all. `Free and cheap` became my new buzzword so to speak- in order to fill in the gaps of time when I was not otherwise busy with everyday living stuff. Then after one more quick rethink I literally had to embark on a new strategy; and engage with an independent financial assistance company- in order to move forward effectively with all of my creditors. Eventually, an informal arrangement was reached- and I could breathe a sigh of relief!

OMG!!!!!! How terribly more difficult my life was about to get- the endless list of wants went on and on! My first lavish expense to forgo was to be my perfume, instead I had to rely on cheaper versions of various toilettes instead. I really had to drastically revamp my lifestyle. I came to enjoy gentle walking exercise as opposed to full on gym sessions or trips to the swimming pool. Personal fitness had always been a priority to me- and I came to be somewhat relieved that I couldn`t any longer go on my cycle either- least of all I couldn`t afford the upkeep on it; and these days it had started to rust in my backyard; becoming a rather expensive garden ornament. So I was in a rather sought after area living a bit of a poor lifestyle; and stick out like a sore thumb I did. Transport became a big issue since I had to on foot it most places; taking ever more exercise to avoid the rising petrol costs. I couldn`t afford to take taxis as frequently as I used to any longer. What really struck me was how people were in fact around this part of town very own transport orientated; and nearly everyone owned a private motor car. My trainers became a staple for me; and I couldn`t believe the footwear I was getting through! Also it wasn`t like back home whereby your friend would offer you a lift for instance. Oh no people around this end of town were mean- they simply wouldn`t have you in their car. In short there was no sense of community. Which I think is why this lead to the eventual closure of the disco nightclubs too. There had been so many complaints, mainly from Church groups; who condemned our devil dancing? They didn`t care that we were out there socialising. They simply didn`t understand; and why didn`t we go elsewhere really. Even complaining about the actual noise generated from the disco parties?! How the face of a city had radically changed overnight! Clubbing culture was undervalued; and blamed somewhat because they as a community wanted to exercise more control over events/ people. It was soooo strange- pubs became then the new voodoo- they were willing to entertain what I considered to be a very boring pubculture- whereby one is forced to sit still for quite a lengthy time and consume vast quantities of alcohol; talking a load of rubbish really! Hahahahahahaha Not really my idea of fun! I became a big fan of a quaint little chocolate box coffee shop- which always filled me with romantic notions especially as I sipped on my hot drink whilst gazing out of the window. It was nice to have company occasionally too; just to have a hot drink and a bit of a catchup; and feel enlightened and empowered by this. These small snippets of conversation once more guided me onwards- enough to plan effectively what I was doing with real depth and meaning. In one whole chat sitting I could redefine my whole life with greater clarity and self-respect. The added problem was pining anyone down too; since by this stage we were all caught up with our own lives in some shape or form. I really had to consider my friendship/ family circle group. And I was pleased to say that I was still blessed. Here I was now with a lot of my own private company time on my hands. Whilst I had to give others their individual space. I really had to get to grips with my own individual needs and how to be fulfilled. Crikey woman! I was well and truly on my own with this conundrum! Hahahahahaha For the first time I had to over ride both boredom, lonliness/isolation. As well as being older in years. This proved to be a task of real skill; and I didn`t want to end up as a badger on the telephone (basically my definition of someone who never seems to get off the phone- and is so reliant on feeding off others). Tranquility was really wanting to reach a fine balancing act now- on one hand as much as I enjoyed some time to be both private and relax; I liked the noise pollution occasionally- except when it became a little intrusive of sorts! It became a nightmare on times leading to all manner of problems.

Self-care becoming another key term high on my agenda.

Well I became the next `Marie Antoinette` of the United Kingdom it would seem- and soon to be beheaded! OMG! I became very good at amassing great amounts of credit in order to support and supplement my lifestyle- and of course hoping and waiting for the next `break` whereby I would aim to make a small fortune of sorts. What did I do? Well I took everyone shopping it would seem! Hahahahahaha. This was my favourite past time when I was not busy. I remained a bit of an old maid- and new my time had passed for marrying purposes. There was just no way in hell that I was going to get married at this stage; despite holding onto my youthful goodlooks! One must add further how I had indeed bedded a string of lovers over the years; and why should I settle? Especially in `these` modern times! Hahahahahaha Besides why should I answer to any man? As much as often I would be filled with the romantic notions of lust coupled with the sense of foreverness- and raised another question: would I really want to share my entire living space/apartment with someone 24hrs 7 days a week? Quite frankly I can well see the need for having separate living quarters back in the day- having analysed in great detail the mansion/castle layouts from historical pasts whereby the Queen would indeed have separate bed chamber from the ruling King. Yes indeed, it made perfect sense to me: for then my private living space allowing me to be as messy as I want to be- still Hahahahahaha, and serving the purpose of allowing me to be seen in public always at my best! (Or at least this is the general principal at least) Hahahahahahaha. For there were times when I would run about scantily clad and dischevelled- which always caused a bit of a stir with the locals! Hahahahahaha. Afterall I was only human- and didn`t feel the need to implement the use of makeup on a daily basis! I just sometimes felt the need not to be over dressed too! There was always a lot of fuss- surrounding how I dressed; as well as my bathing rituals came under scrutiny once more. Hey man, I still use moisturisers and purfumes- what the fuck is your problem?! Naturally I continue to have body odour- I`d be worried if I didn`t! Some weird people had recommended that I have armpit sweat gland therapy?!- Hey no way man- it just interferes with the whole biological homeostasis theory in my view. Sweating is good for the heart; an indication of a good workout. Some fools were still subscribing to machines- in order to work out- okay whatever floats your boat! In my days they called that cheating! Hahahahahaha.

I guess what i`m saying is how my whole lifestyle had completely dictated now that I was still very much a single woman! But what I enjoyed more than anything was in fact the freedom to do as I please- I could literally do whatever I wanted, whenever I wanted! And this I know pissed a lot of people off! But hey I wasn`t about to explain myself either to anyone, or apologise for looking after myself. When I was 16 years I didn`t want to be the one wishing they could do it all over again- or live through someone else let`s say!

Well it was not an easy road to go onwards with- since I missed Warren immensely so; everyday in fact! And then as if by magic I entered into another commonlaw marriage of sorts. Of coarse we both wanted each other- I hasten to add; and he is blonde and beautiful. The car visa shade screen concealed his eyes for the first time- and he basically spoke the much needed words: "...Get ready to be by wedded wife!". From years gone by no one in my opinion can dictate terms of enagagement so to speak to anyone really. For just to echo those old ancient words of the past how- one cannot truly stand in the way of true love! We got married just before the weekend too! And soon enough he as in my bed- oh how we cannot wait to romp! Hahahahahahaha. It`s why we continue to truly love each other; and now know each other intimately so to speak, in terms of my ways very much indeed! Hahahahahaaha. Anyway our wedding was very low key, and a marriage of secret really. I just had to know- and dared to ask the burning question of: did he love me? And he certainly does! Hahahahahahaha. There were one or two in the viallage whom dared to contest our marriage- and challenge it everyday it seemed. But who were they? To stand in our way- as far as I was concerned they were indeed jealous. I never hid my dark past- in fact it came to a point whreby I couldn`t any longer. And it was time to face up to as the judge put it- should I do it again- I would surely face imprinsonment! I had indeed made a lot of enemeies through breaking with my dark past. And cause me problems they would still pursue me for their own ends. I was nowadays doing a great job of continuing on with my cleaned up lifestyle. This was the city- and as I made an ongoing lifestyle choice- I was determined to make it clear how: I owe you nothing! Simply I was getting on with my life- and now everything I had hoped and dreamed of was coming my way babe! Hahahahahahaha. Of coarse I remained confident in my looks and my abilities enough to secure a reasonably good standard of life. It was afterall admittedly what I had described during my teens- and now I was satisfied of the actual wait in progress- and relieved that I ad not chosen to marry the first man- in my teens! Things kind of took shape when I made a conscious decision not to return to my home village; but instead to relocate to a suburb in the city- of coarse in order to meet my `match` so to speak.

Still I couldn`t drive for economic and health reasons- so almost all of my outdoor pursuits were on foot. And today how I longed for a new pair of trainers! I simply went through footwear like lightening- and the treads on my current trainers were through! I just this evening threw no less than four pairs of shoes away! Hahahahahaha. I would enjoy a taxi ride occasionally too; depending on finance and distance. The recent price increases really took their toll- did this fuel/spark our marriage? Absolutely not! We were two people very much in love! It was and continues to be very much the world versus US! Hahahahahahha. And I really didn`t care what others had to say- with their stupid comments. After some threatening intimidation antics- I quite simply grew stronger again- and refused to give up my husband for anyone. The opposition came largely from what is rather nicely termed: the dark web! I basically nowadays refer to it as sewer rats and scum largely. The unpleasant dealings with `that` lot over the years had taught me to keep safe really- and not to take my personal safety for granted.

Every so often I felt his big arms around me, he provided a constant source of comfort and everlasting love- which was indeed `forever`. Never did I feel lonely; for I knew my husband was always around me. He may not have been roses- but when he kissed me and loved me too- he was absolutely everything I needed and wanted. It was certainly give and take in our marriage- and I loved and still live for seeing his handsome face; for this is enough!

Well it would seem how upon discovering our soon and rather quickly carried out marriage- it was very quickly annulled by a good friend. Another shock for me- for this was to be our second time round go at marriage. I realised then he was indeed a fool! Especially since he tried to pretend how: money didn`t matter! Hahahahahahaha. Anyway after a few damns and blasts; twas better that I came to realise this sooner than later. What a most Royal cockup! And it had indeed created quite a stir amongst the local soldiers. But you know what they say: a silver lining in every cloud! Hahahahaha. Firstly I needed this damage to be irreversible- for my own heartsake. Meaning that I did not care to take him back again under any circumstances this time if it was to be over- it would indeed be over for good! I was still a relatively young woman and needed to move forward. Besides I had seen a side to him that I didn`t care for. How on earth could he have behaved so badly towards me? I then reached the conclusion that he was out of his fuckin` mind. And so couldn`t stomach him any longer. It just grated badly nowadays with me. This wasn`t a boyfriend of sorts- this was a complete tosser in my estimation- which didn`t really count for much these days since my very association with him was bringing me down in the greater society. And indeed whilst his goodlooks were what attracted me to him- he was to `me` an ugly person! Oh the humiliation- this was not love?! And whilst I remained blessed in my personal qualities- I still needed love on my terms uttermost. Not simply when the mood took him!

It would appear how Romeo Zane who I had not had dealings with for some time stepped into the breach. Quite unexpectedly. And once more all sanity was saved! This saved me from much despair and upset- and positively I was used to it all `going to cock` nowadays; and learned how he wasn`t for me. Yes I had indeed been messed around enough over they years. I then had to quickly take stock of my life once more- and realise that he would only ever be a glorified sperm donor- for all intents and purposes. And was resolved to heartbreak numero uno ! For reference purposes I was able to draw on this firsthand dark experience- and quickly cheered up afterwards. Would I and could I ever love another man? Hell yes! Easilly so in fact from my past history; particularly in my time spent in the Channel islands; otherwise known as heartbreak island! Hahahahahahaha. Oh how we drank and married. This bastard couldn`t even bring himself to do anything romantic pretty much! Hahahahahahaha. Oh how easily I severed all ties with what was a pile of shite really! They hated it when I eventually gave them something real! Hahahahahahaha

Would I consider marriage again?! Hell no! Hahahahahahahahaha- perhaps not so readily! I was sooooo sick of trying to sell myself to a rather stupid man- for what message came carried back was that he simply wanted to live in a tent! I mean a `tent` really. It was then I realised the height of his supidity- for he truly imagined that he could live on love alone!? In this economic climate. The wolves were at everyones` door. And I have never been soooo relieved to have been effectively saved by Romeo Zane- who`s name I thought I would never speak again! Hahahahahahahaha

Anyway, what I didn`t plan for-was indeed everyone finding out! I had my suspicions for rather a while; but how on earth do you propose to challenge someone that supposedly knows that indeed Warren and I were having an affair?! The point is I never did- and it would certainly account for much of the social hostility that I was facing right now from one or two wierdos. This created an extra problem in itself from the very fact that they were interfering in our `relationship` whether I liked it or not! I could not believe the sheer amount of nosey parkers that really were intrigued by my private life?! It would seem; our relationship created many an unwanted problem/crime in itself. Fortunately Warren and I were in fact big enough to both look after ourselves. The main motive of these sordid people was to in fact not only challenge our relationship- on the grounds of suggesting that due to my mental health condition- I was not all there!? Slanderous gossips continued to somewhat plague our lives also thinking that they could effectively bribe us both- and try to gain a financial incentive from our ongoing turmoil- that was our relationship! Hahahahahaha. I couldn`t believe it when after a considerable amount of trouble from these rather persistant lobby-activists- and it became a scenario of: Nowhere to run to baby, no where to hide! As the famous song lyrics spring to mind! Hahahahahaha. Warren did eventually come to `visit` me one evening to basically say how: we had indeed been discovered! And basically said: "... they now know that me and you are having an affair..."! It was soooooo nice to at last see him that evening- and the rather grand gesture that he made if not a little `rude`, was indeed a welcome unexpected declaration of his love towards me! Hahahahahahaha

Just when life became a little more awkward- in terms of-how does one actually spot a 'lover' of sorts?! Well it turns out to be a lot easier than one originally anticipated it would seem! Hahahahahahaha. For it just takes 1 or 2 individuals to 'find out' and Bobs` your uncle! All hell breaks loose and little unwanted/unpolite occurances happen. Low and behold- things came to a 'crunch' it would seem . And wait `til one gets all manner of cretins round to one`s home address. As yet another lover appears to want to teach me a lesson it would seem. This ongoing battle coupled with that of the dark web- and avoiding the prostitution gangs like the plague. I knew only to well how this simply held no future. In addition I really had to consider my future with Warren- or perhaps without him. For both myself and Warren grew distant and evermore apart. Strangely I did not become overly upset due to how my overall outlook on life had much improved as they years went by. I just thought well really I should be aiming a little higher in the marriage market- especially with my qualifications, good looks and substance as a woman. I was indeed very much enjoying my single status. And then it was like when 2 buses come along together at the same time! Hahahahahahaha. And I had grown tired of his ongoing bullshit basically; as well as his enormous attitude problem. I then had to place a little self value in myself once more- and I felt very empowered by this. Both lovers by this time knew about the other it would seem. And so I made a deeply considered choice to basically ditch Warren; because I could stand the fighting no more- if not the long silence from him which was deafening at this point in time. He became a non-stop excuse man and complainer of things which I knew he was being utterly unreasonable and horrid! It was most certainly time to try a new lover!

My infatuation and obsession for this new man who was indeed making himself known to me- and yes the attraction was there as soon as we set eyes upon each other. I knew things were moving slowly- so as to avoid being on the rebound so to speak and therefore making oneself too open in terms of being hurt in the process! He continued to shower me with compliments- and then Warren knew I was indeed leaving him! (once more). But I must stay true to myself here- and I simply refuse to marry beneath me- for I now realise this would simply not work well- when considering my happiness as a mature, educated, head strong, comfortable in one`s own body woman. I liked how this new lover was making himself known to me- and I indeed in turn returned the hot pursuit! Hahahahahahahaha. I had become the grandmaster of breakups by this time too! Hahahahahahahaha. Always realising how it was important not to blame myself- just that we were indeed too different. I soon discovered how my own personal ambition would always swamp things- and Warren was just too immature for me really- if not dull. Besides I loathed his past time pursuits. Our lives were just worlds apart and way too different at this time. Warren still took pleasure in cheapmans` holidays to turkey, with cheap beer; and you can guess the rest.....(cheap tarts). Whereas I on the other hand preferring sophistication and cultural breaks to Paris!

Another unusual chapter in my life begun all over again- the utter pottyness of well `living` really; as well as adapting to change. And making the best of potentially bad and hazardess situations! Crikey! Just trying to re-house a 'nutter mun' anywhere within the city still proving to be a nightmare waiting to happen on times! (people seriously with no care for psychiatric service users believing that they could in effect- move me on- and simply get rid of me- the lengths they went to- what a mess/and utter disgrace!). Since there was widespread opposition- openly displayed in aggressive ways too! All sorts of stories/slanderous on times were indeed created just to make life a little more difficult and awkward for people like myself. I found myself in a series of ongoing engagements/meetings of sorts with psychiatric services; consequently myself being most pivotal in the entire communication process and thus leading to-'no concerns currently' about my goodself. I found myself back in the loving arms of Mr Zane- our relationship was also one of co-dependancy- I needed him and I knew he needed me!- softly/gently I knew what I was doing- oh absolutely- since Mr Zane showed me 'people' in the process of getting up close and personal with them- and everytime I ran a bloody mile! Hahahahahahaha- I saw the flaws in people only too well- not that I was overly judging them- but Mr Zane was and remains a hard man to follow/match! Particularly our living standards- and what was acceptable for me- well obviously wasn't doable for others! I was an intelligent and capable woman leading an extraordinary life-with no room for 'gutter rats'! Quite simply they were -'cut –throats' and of coarse I naturally distanced myself from this sort of carry-on; for to safeguard me being a victim 'again'!

As much as it was not daunting but inconvenient to effectively interrupt my life in order to liase effectively in these minor matters of both concern and aggravation. I particularly enjoyed receiving this good feedback. Although life is not easy- it's exactly how you deal with it is what matters really. I continue to digest my living circumstances from day to day and strive for better things/achievements- after all only I have the power to change this!

How on earth did I cope with the perceived 'bad' behaviour of others? Well it was a learning process of tactics/skill and gave a 'talking point' on times for sure! Hahahahahaha- I just found some peoples' behaviour really weird! Naturally I followed advice from professionals as well as much needed guidance with adopting coping strategies. I was also sending a clear message: My life was not open for negotiation; as they really had it 'in' for me. It was most promising to focus upon positive thoughts- and 'No' I refuse to listen to those I perceive to be attempting to control me/my life really! I continued to mingle with the best of them though

I`m pleased to say; the student population is where I continued to thrive. Not just exist or live- but to thrive with a most enriched life indeed. It would appear how these people who constantly opposed me as a human being- really wanted what I had! Which is why I was resigned to think on times how these people were really stupid- and no way would I be taken over by them! Hahahahahahahaha. For who one earth conforms to slavery these days in a modern Great Britain?! Only the vulnerable and those lacking something I suppose! I still consider myself a very empowered woman these days with my abusers still at large in society- for they still know not what they did! And this is my lesson in itself for we reap what we sow in terms of considering ambition as an unwavering `rock of ages`! For I knew and grasped the importance of ambition early on- then there was a lot more to learn in between and in the meantime. Like I did not take the news well of an educated lecturer in Paris recently being attacked basically- because of who he was, and what he stood for- which in itself is `education`. So now that said it just really highlighted the importance of health and safety even more so for me. And thankfully being a control freak was a bonus! Because I quite simply have capacity and am able to represent/display my individual free-will and determination.

One thing I had most definitely learned over the years was how Mr Zane could never be trusted again really. For today he came to tell me how his latest fancy woman and him had completely finished? How did I fit into all this? Well I didn`t really! I was really surprised that he even still spoke to me- given some time to ponder on this. I really was not going to go down that road again- life is far too short- and I need to be loved not betrayed all over again in order to make him feel good! I did at first feel a degree of sympathy perhaps and then I kind of pinched myself- and short of banging my own head against a wall hyperthetically which would be kinder really! Hahahahahahaha. I had played Mr Zane`s deadly games for long enough now to know that I needed/wanted to cut my loses before all hell broke loose once more. He had a inept way of causing chaos with a string of women. Nowadays; I was no longer mad with him or angry in that sense. For I couldn't believe how he actually had the cheek to think I would entertain him once more on any romantic level- the realist in me kicked in and quickly too! Hahahahahahaha. I simply could not allow myself to harbour any further feelings of love or otherwise towards him at this stage- besides it simply was not fair! He was indeed being cruel to be kind? I had enough of being the butt of his jokes really. It was time to appreciate everything I had achieved and the viscious insulting games continued like never before. It was a mixture of hatism versus controlism as well as an all out popularity contest in itself! Hahahahahahaha. No one understood of coarse better than me! And why should they after all they had lives of their own surely?! It would appear the entire community was once more in my business! Much for the devilment of the participants in gossip. I came to appreciate once more how some people will never understand! And why should they!? Afterall as I entered another phase of my relationship with Warren I simply cared not what others though at all! We did it for ourselves ultimately! The more we were forced apart- the further we fought to remain together! Not all respected how I had a private life- the worst culprits I simply erased permananently from my life therafterwards. Me now speaking Italiano! Hahahahahahaha- in the sense that yeah whatever- leave them get on with it- and then we are free to enjoy ourselves- and do as we please really- not everyone grasped this though. Here I was a grown woman with thoughts/ideas and a life of my own- indeed my mental health condition would always be there- however it didn't change anything in the grand scheme of things. As their vulgar behaviour/s continued to come to the fore- quietly it just served further as an indication of how seriously confused they were! For once more they were simply going out of their way to upset me-and whilst in my condition/state of pregnancy. May they fight on.......for I had reached the stage of how it was all too apparent- Warren cares alright! Hence exactly why I am having HIS baby! It was quite embarrassing really for them-for I knew I did not need to act like a fool really.

I always recall how: it`s nice to be nice! And how everything comes out in the wash! In short a game of great skill and tactics too. I just continued to play my cards right! Oh absolutely! And for the first time opened and felt safe to open the channels of discussion too- addressing matters like psychosis- as well as other encountered problems. Confidence building it wasn`t- these people were spoiling for a fight once more- I was used to their shinanigans- this time it was different indeed! After I had gotten rid/lost the Religious cult, and the drug barons and the sewer rats/ex girlfriends the list went onwards- I was well placed as a glowing socialite once more complete with an army of friends too! Nothing was holding me back- nor would I be mentally imprisoned by their backwards jealous thinking! The partite continued- basically an organisation of people whom just had an alternate and better way of life- we were indeed people who knew what we wanted and exactly how to achieve this! In fact people looked up to us and respected us for this. I always knew how I was better than causing affront unnecessarily- for I was educated!!!!!! This went a long way believe me- I had got my image back- my credibility- the works! And more besides! And what`s more with my fine sports` womans` physique etc- the entire fucking community was talking again! Hahahahahahahaah

Well what a complete and utter turn around- perhaps not so; for at the start of the day I was prewarned how- the start of world war III was soon to be upon us. And I really wish that my ex boyfriend of sorts Mr Zane would indeed keep me out of his current relationships/affairs. That said I was the object of much scrutiny and dissatisfaction again- since this was thrust upon me once more that I was indeed having an affair with Mr Zane?! Not so- but I can see how it served its excuseful purpose- crikey- what a cheap shot! There is no love lost between myself and Mr Zane any longer- there will be no rekindling of romantic affections. I by this stage had managed to build a life for myself. And I was rather surprised to see that most of my day actually had been quite involved in Mr Zanes` trifling mind! Hahahahahahaaha. Where did I come into it?! Well quite simply- I didn`d- nor did I care to.

Since my ex boyfriends continued there smear campaign of trifling in my life whenever it suited them. I quietly looked to pursue relationships elsewhere.

Recently I had come to notice how we were an entirely separate group of people- I`m not suggesting 'better' than that old lot- however I certainly came to prefer my new lifestyle and social group. I just needed to explore logic and sense making!? That old lot were a bit of a tribal existence; neither they or myself were prepared to ompromise in terms of setting out how one wants to live. Still very much a realist- now they sought something which I had/possessed not the other way round. What I was recognising was how we were now indeed worlds apart especially when considering things like social mobility. And whilst I was upwards- I was all to reluctant to go downwards again!? And why should I- to suit others- not so- for I well rememeber how they rather enjoyed a kick about with my head in the past. I was determined to be successful and affluent. As opposed to poor and no prospects in life- without due motivation etc. I much preferred life today- as opposed to the dark old days – and I can tell you that they simply set out from the outset to help themselves! And why not! I remained a successful woman in modern times- still moving with the times/era. I still had my mum to remind me of olden days gone by whereby women were lucky to have a washing machine!? Thank god those days are over!!!!!!!! Still looking for love proved tricky especially with some ex boyfriends still around! But at least it cleared all confusion once more in knowing that I harboured no feelings for him any longer. For I would have to be a prized pratt to enjoy being upset surely?! Thank God I had long departed from that cult effectively. And god help you if you were found to be not pretty!? I don`t know but i'd had enough of quality control and their sub standards as to dictate what constitutes good-looking! In comparison to former boyfriend-material I had acquired a far better taste. Or so I thought! I just simply had to agree with the long and distant Cleopatra theory- since I was not only admired for my looks but also for how I spoke- in certain parts. In short I now did everything to avoid the cult; I did not wish to aspire to be a stupid heir priestess of sorts! And found them to be rather insulting towards intelligent and capable women like myself! My my – when a cult goes all out to be jealous of my friends, family and you name it- they set out to categorically destroy me and my life for I refused to return to them! It was vitally important to put as much distance away from myself and this religious cult as possible- I was concerned regarding their recruitment stategies involving illicit drugs as well as other dark web activities. They preyed on successful people. Their antics were absolutely out of this world! Like you wouldn't believe- they were again sending another message- you will not ignore us! I knew I had to save myself basically for those who remained- were there by choice- there simply was no room for me- partly because I was a free-thinking woman and I was not going to comply to a backwards cult. I channelled my distant memories once more- and run basically like a good-'un! Hahahahahahaha. Knowing that I was unable and couldn't save anyone else from this cult- it was tragic really for they became so entrenched in their beliefs and shabby way of life- they were on the road to no where- they also were in dire states of poverty. Yet they could not help themselves- nor did they want to escape- you could effectively waste an entire age trying to help someone else who really would be wasting your time. They were quite good at commanding sympathy however this is not to be confused with drawing you in effectively. For they needed you to need them- this is indeed the first mistake of overpowering an individual. When they saw how I was not receptive to this and so would often rebel in the past before leaving the cult- I was not only banished but hunted effectively by this cult movement.

I therefore did continue my participation with my roman catholic faith- however- it was in good measure and in a positive and healthy fashion. It did not disclude me from God and fellow worshipers and practising my faith around celebratory times including Christmas for instance. Yes babe- I was on the run once more- from more than just a handful of disgruntled personas from the past; and now a cult too!

www.ingramcontent.com/pod-product-compliance
Ingram Content Group UK Ltd.
Pitfield, Milton Keynes, MK11 3LW, UK
UKHW040058140125
453557UK00001B/138